WARNING!

THIS BOOK HAS LOADS OF VERY DISGUSTING MONSTERS IN IT!

Hairy ones, smelly ones, fat ones, oozy ones. None of them are very nice, and they study the Monsterbook to become more not very nice.

... by monsters, for monsters. A filthy, fact-packed handbook to everything monster!

Michael Broad spent much of his childhood gazing out of the window imagining he was somewhere more interesting. Now he's a grown-up, Michael still spends a lot of time gazing out of the window imagining he's somewhere more interesting – but these days he writes and illustrates books as well.

Books by Michael Broad

MONSTERBOOK: PONGDOLLOP AND THE SCHOOL STINK
MONSTERBOOK: SNOTGOBBLE AND THE BOGEY BULLY

JAKE CAKE: THE FOOTBALL BEAST
JAKE CAKE: THE PIRATE CURSE
JAKE CAKE: THE ROBOT DINNER LADY
JAKE CAKE: THE SCHOOL DRAGON
JAKE CAKE: THE VISITING VAMPIRE
JAKE CAKE: THE WEREWOLF TEACHER

MONSTERBOOK

Snotgobble and the Bogey Bully

MICHAEL BROAD

PUFFIN

PUFFIN BOOKS

Published by the Penguin Group
Penguin Books Ltd, 80 Strand, London WC2R 0RL, England
Penguin Group (USA) Inc., 375 Hudson Street, New York, New York 10014, USA
Penguin Group (Canada), 90 Eglinton Avenue East, Suite 700, Toronto, Ontario, Canada M4P 2Y3 (a division of Pearson Penguin Canada Inc.)
Penguin Ireland, 25 St Stephen's Green, Dublin 2, Ireland (a division of Penguin Books Ltd)
Penguin Group (Australia), 250 Camberwell Road, Camberwell, Victoria 3124, Australia (a division of Pearson Australia Group Pty Ltd)
Penguin Books India Pvt Ltd, 11 Community Centre, Panchsheel Park, New Delhi – 110 017, India
Penguin Group (NZ), 67 Apollo Drive, Rosedale, North Shore 0632, New Zealand (a division of Pearson New Zealand Ltd)
Penguin Books (South Africa) (Pty) Ltd, 24 Sturdee Avenue, Rosebank, Johannesburg 2196, South Africa

Penguin Books Ltd, Registered Offices: 80 Strand, London WC2R 0RL, England

puffinbooks.com

First published 2009
1

Set in Perpetua
Made and printed in England by Clays Ltd, St Ives plc

British Library Cataloguing in Publication Data
A CIP catalogue record for this book is available from the British Library

ISBN: 978–0–141–32454–8

CONTENTS

FLESHBLOB DETAILS

NAME .... Will ....

ADDRESS .... 33 Highland Road ....

this book belongs to URK
MONSTERBOOK
WELCOME TO THE REVOLTING WORLD OF THE MONSTERBOOK! THE GRISLY GUIDE TO ALL THINGS MONSTER!
Whether you're hideously hairy, terrifyingly tentacled, creepily clawed or just a great big mess of disgustingness, Monsterbook has everything you need for a career in fear.
This book comes with the name and address of your allocated fleshblob FOR SCARE-TRAINING PURPOSES!

THIS IS URK

Urk is a monster.
But to his parents' disappointment he's not very scary.

When Urk began *scare training* with the MONSTERBOOK he made friends with Will, his allocated fleshblob!

THIS IS WILL

Will is a human.
He thinks monsters are revolting, but also very interesting.

SCARE TRAINING

When Urk's meant to be out *scaring* Will, the pair watch TV, eat *snacks* and read the MONSTERBOOK.
Urk makes up weekly *scare reports* for his parents, and Will learns more about the disgusting world of Monsterland.

MONSTERLAND

Monsterland is the underground world where monsters live. It's very dirty, smelly and lit by thousands of stolen light bulbs.

Earthy tunnels lead to the human world above, where monsters enter through secret doorways – hidden under beds, behind curtains and inside wardrobes...

1

Miffni the Mean

In his murky brown bedroom, Urk shoved the *Monsterbook* into his rucksack and headed for the door. It was a scare-training night and the young monster was looking forward to spending time with his fleshblob friend Will.

Unfortunately his path was blocked by something large and mean.

'Where do you think you're going?' growled Miffni, folding her arms defiantly.

Miffni was technically Urk's *little* sister – being two years younger – but she was twice his size and much more frightening.

'Scare training, of course!' said Urk, trying to nudge his way past.

'Oh yes,' she sneered, still refusing to budge. 'I forgot about all those fantastic scare reports you fill out every week. You probably think you've got Mum and Dad completely fooled.'

'I have no idea what you're talking about,' sighed Urk.

'Really?' said Miffni, producing a brown paper bag and waving it at him. 'Then you must have a very good excuse for these,' she added, tipping the contents over his head.

Urk's eyes widened as the empty

snack wrappers fluttered down around him and landed at his hooves. They were not Monsterland snack wrappers from Hairballs or Bugs' Legs – these were all wrappers from fleshblob snacks!

'Where did you get those?' he gasped.

'I've been snooping through your rucksack looking for proof that you're up to something,' Miffni stated proudly. 'And now I have evidence that you've been raiding your fleshblobs' food cupboards!'

'So what if I have?' Urk said quickly, relieved that she didn't suspect anything more. Stealing food *was* forbidden while in training – due to the obvious risks of rummaging around a kitchen. But making friends with a fleshblob was the worst thing a monster could do. 'It's none of your business anyway!' he added.

'You're right,' said Miffni. 'But it *is* Mum and Dad's business.'

'You're going to *tell* on me?' Urk gasped, quickly gathering up the evidence.

'Actually, I already have,' grinned Miffni, jabbing a chubby thumb in the direction of the living room. 'Mum and

Dad sent me to fetch you. And they don't look very happy . . .'

2

The Bogey Bully

'BOO!' said Urk, jumping from the wardrobe and plonking his rucksack on Will's cluttered desk. The young monster seemed in a hurry and didn't collapse into his usual beanbag in front of the TV.

'ARGH!' said Will. 'What's up?'

'My sister has been going through my stuff and found some old crisp bags and biscuit wrappers!' Urk gasped. 'She's convinced my parents that I've been slacking off scare training and that I spend the whole time stealing snacks!'

'Uh oh!' said Will, knowing how mean Urk's enormous little sister was.

'That's not the worst of it,' Urk sighed. He reached into his rucksack, pulled out a small glossy catalogue and handed it to his friend. 'My parents have decided to take me off nightly scare training and they're making me do *this* instead.'

What had looked like a glossy catalogue was actually a *dull* catalogue covered in slime, so the boy took the corner with the tips of his fingers and held it up.

'What is it?' Will gasped, thinking it looked like a catalogue selling humans.

FLESHBLOB SUIT

Very realistic human disguise. Fleshblob suits were invented to allow monsters to sneak above ground and scare flesh-blob children during the day when they least expect it.

'It's the latest line of rubber fleshblob suits,' Urk explained. 'My parents want me to switch to daytime scares, disguised

as a human. I'm supposed to choose one from the catalogue and pick it up tonight.'

'Tonight?' Will sighed, not wanting to spend a boring evening alone.

'Yeah,' said Urk and began rummaging in his rucksack. Eventually he pulled out a dirty brown sack and a pair of forks and waved them at Will. 'Fancy a trip to Monsterland?'

'Definitely!' said Will. The Jub Jub disguise meant the boy could enter the tunnels and mingle among monsters without any of them knowing he was a fleshblob, which was exciting and terrifying all at the same time.

Before pulling on the Jub Jub disguise, Will couldn't resist looking through the *Fleshblob Fantasia* catalogue. He was surprised how many different themes there were in the contents page, from 'Dreadful Dinner Ladies' to 'Not Nice Nannies', although they all had *something* to do with children.

'Have you chosen one?' asked Will, flicking to the 'Tyrant Teachers' section.

‘Not yet,’ said Urk, peering over the boy’s shoulder.

All the fleshblob suits in the ‘Tyrant Teachers’ section had long noses and fierce expressions on their faces. The male ones wore beige suits with patches on their elbows and the female ones wore floral dresses and cardigans.

TYRANT TEACHERS

MR MEANIE: He loves nothing more than a daily maths quiz!

MRS GRIM: She'll bake plain *sugar-free* cookies for the class.

MRS MOAN: She'll hand out *stale* sweets covered in fluff!

MR GRUEL: He comes with a free red pen for all those F's!

'You think I should get one of *those*?' asked Urk, frowning at the teachers.

'No, I was just checking to see if any of my teachers were in here,' laughed Will. 'Some of them are pretty monstrous, so I wouldn't be surprised if they were monsters in disguise.'

Urk took the catalogue and flicked to the 'Naughty Kids' section.

'I was thinking of going for one of these,' he said, holding up the page full of boys and girls around Will's age. 'They're more my

size and I thought if I looked like a regular kid we could hang out during the daytime.'

Will's eyes grew wide and his mouth dropped open.

'What's the matter?' asked Urk. 'Don't you think that sounds fun?'

'That kid just started at my school!' gasped Will, pointing to one of the larger boy suits named Terrible Tyler. 'He's not in my year, but he steals *everyone's* food at break time. He's the reason I couldn't offer you any snacks this week.'

'I wondered why that was,' said Urk, taking a closer look at the description.

'What else can you tell me about this boy?' asked Urk, putting the catalogue aside and picking up the *Monsterbook*. 'If we can work out what kind of monster is under the suit, we might be able to find his weaknesses.'

'All I know is that if anyone refuses to hand over their food, he smears them with massive bogeys,' said Will, shuddering at the memory. 'Something he seems to have an endless supply of.'

'An endless supply of bogeys, eh?' asked Urk, turning to the 'Gruesome Gallery' in the *Monsterbook*. The 'Gruesome Gallery' contains every kind of monster known to monster and after flicking between a few likely snotty suspects he eventually narrowed it down to one.

'You've got a Goopsnottle on your hands!' Urk gasped.

'URGH!' said Will, checking his hands for Goopsnottles.

'No, one of *these*,' said Urk, tapping the page in the *Monsterbook*.

GOOPSNOTTLE

Goopsnottles are aggressive, disgusting and have a very sweet tooth. They favour intimidation and looting over traditional scaring and usually seek out a regular source of sweet food.

Natural defences include bogey smearing, bogey flicking, and the manufacture of bogey bombs. Goopsnottles are very territorial and always work alone.

WEAKNESSES: They have no weaknesses!

‘URGH!’ said Will when he saw the illustration.

‘So there’s nothing I can do to get rid of him?’ asked Will.

‘Not unless you want to get splattered with bogey bombs,’ said Urk, packing the catalogue and the *Monsterbook*

into his rucksack. 'And from what I've heard, that stuff will stick around for weeks!'

'Monsters are horrible!' said Will, pulling on the Jub Jub sack and poking his forks through the grubby material. He peered through two meshy eyeholes and saw Urk gazing at his hooves. Realizing what he'd said, the boy quickly added, 'Except you, of course!'

'I know you didn't mean me,' sighed Urk, pulling the rucksack on to his shoulders. 'But you're right. The kids

in your school shouldn't have to put up with a greedy Goopsnottle stealing their food.'

'But the *Monsterbook* said they have no weaknesses,' said Will.

'We'll think of something,' said Urk, patting his friend on the shoulder.

Will nodded uncertainly as they stepped into the wardrobe.

Once inside, the pair ducked through the hidden doorway and entered the damp, earthy tunnels leading to Monsterland. Urk pointed out a Nod and a Gwomper among the many creatures scuttling past, and Will looked them up in the *Monsterbook* to take his mind off the bogey bully.

NOD

Nods are sock-eating monsters. They snuffle around under beds and inside laundry baskets - hunting for the most cheesy ones. Nods are not very scary, but losing a sock is very frustrating to fleshblobs.

PANTS: If no socks can be found, a Nod will eat pants instead!

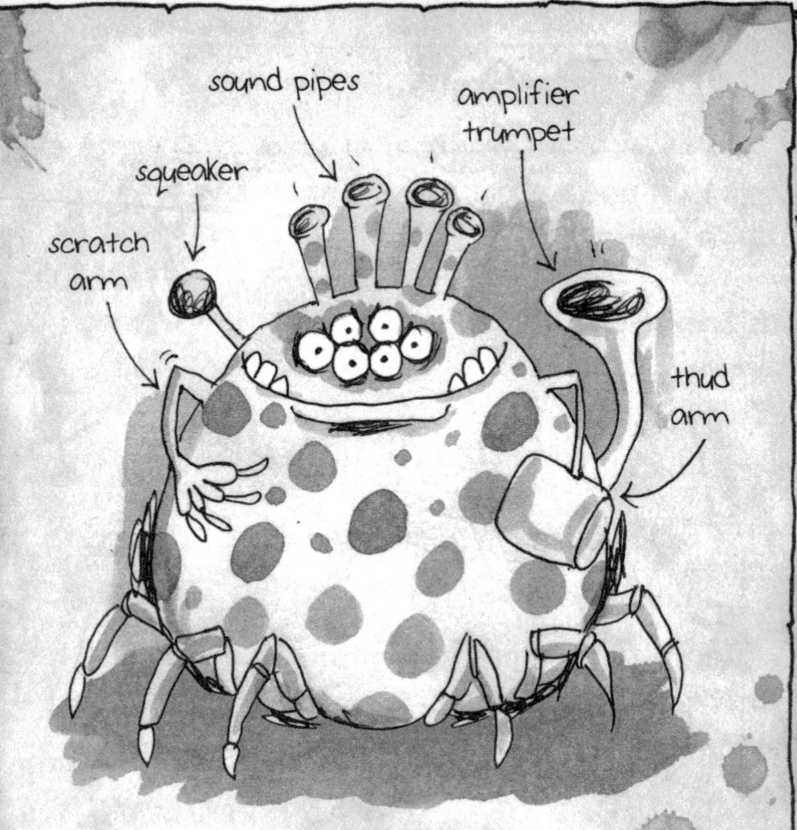

GWOMPER

Gwompers specialize in making scary noises. Most of the sounds a fleshblob can hear in the darkness, like squeaky floorboards, scratching under the bed or an ominous thud, all come from the sound-pipes of a Gwomper.

FART: Gwompers are also very good at fart noises and have their own fart choir!

3

Monster Mall

When Urk and Will stepped out of the tunnels, Monster City spread out before them like a gigantic, steaming dungheap under a murky, starry night. The star

effect came from the thousands of grubby light bulbs stuck in the enormous domed ceiling, and the dungheap effect came from most of the buildings being made of dung.

The pair made their way through the Fungus Forest that surrounded the city and hurried through the Slug Slums – where slugpickers were filling their buckets with slimy slugs to sell at Monster Market. Urk then led Will to a part of Monster City he'd never seen before, and at first the boy thought

he was being taken to see the largest dog poo in the universe.

'Welcome to Monster Mall!' said Urk as they approached the giant dollop.

'Monster City has a *mall*?' Will gasped, stepping through the sliding doors that squelched upon opening. He was always surprised at how similar Monsterland was to the world above, except that almost everything underground was brown and smelled terrible.

'Of course we have a mall,' laughed Urk. 'We're not *savages*!'

Will paused to take in the corkscrew interior and curved escalators leading to different departments. Then he frowned in the direction of a nearby shop called Savage Supplies.

'Oh, that's a supply store for monsters who live in the Outer Regions,' Urk explained. 'I suppose they are *technically* savages, but they still like to visit the city occasionally to do their shopping.'

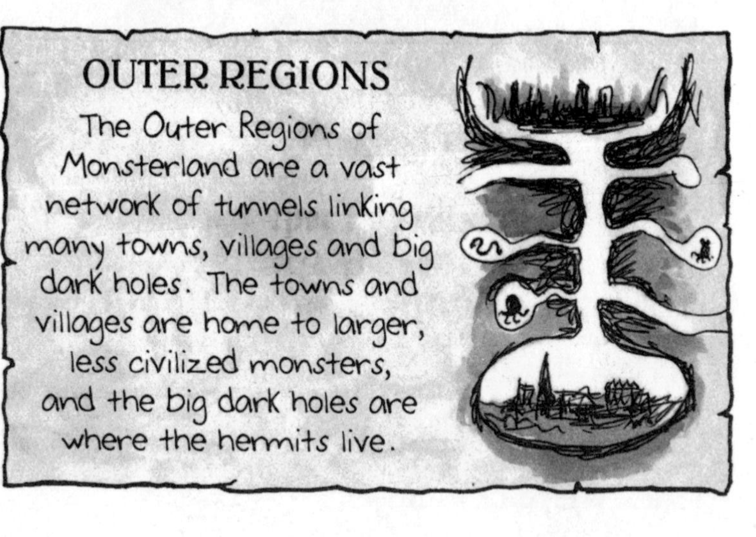

As they made their way through the busy Monster Mall, Will couldn't help staring at all the different shops. There was a toyshop called Little Horrors, full of baby monsters running around with scary toys; a McSlug's restaurant, packed with monsters slobbering over slug-burgers

and worm-sticks; and a cosmetics store called Pretty Putrid, with two thorny monsters plastering their faces with something green and slimy.

Will thought it was odd that Monsterland had a cosmetics store at all, so he took a leaflet from the rack by the door.

As they continued through Monster Mall, Will stopped and peered into Boo's Books, where a hovering Slinky was running a long black finger along the shelves. When the creature turned and grinned at him, the boy hurried away to catch up with Urk. He'd read about Slinkies in the *Monsterbook* and didn't want one following him home!

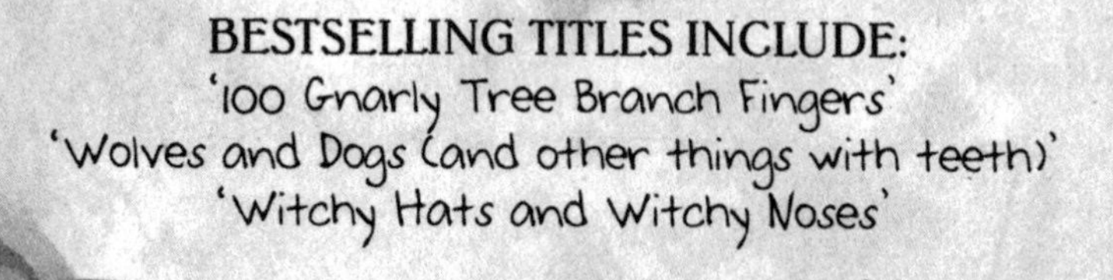

SLINKY

Slinkies are made almost entirely of black smoke, with a couple of eyes and usually a fang or two. This monster can change shape to make scary shadows on the walls of fleshblob bedrooms. Slinkies are not very imaginative, so they study books on scare shapes.

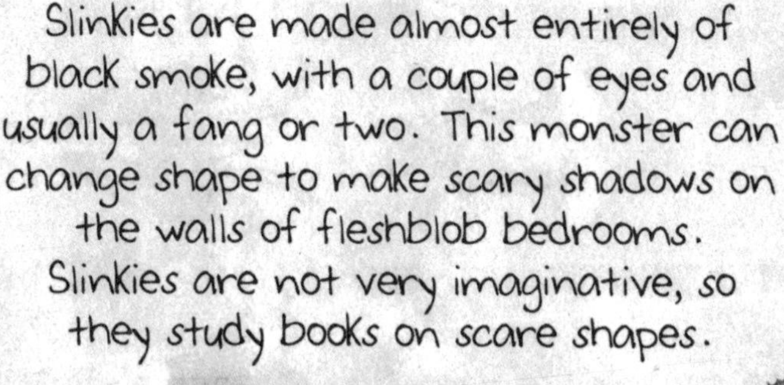

BESTSELLING TITLES INCLUDE:
'100 Gnarly Tree Branch Fingers'
'Wolves and Dogs (and other things with teeth)'
'Witchy Hats and Witchy Noses'

4

Fleshblob Fantasia

Will found Urk standing outside Fleshblob Fantasia, and as they stepped through the doors the boy took one look around and shrieked. It wasn't a loud shriek, it was

more of a high-pitched gasp, but it was enough for Urk to take him aside quickly.

'What's the matter?' Urk whispered.

Will's wide eyes were fixed on the hundreds of fleshblob suits dangling from hangers. The suits weren't actually frightening, but they were incredibly lifelike and seeing so many saggy human skins was quite alarming!

'It's only rubber,' said Urk, lifting

a nearby arm and waving it in the air. The arm belonged to a little old lady suit that was so realistic Will had to fight the urge to wave back so as not to appear rude.

'I'm OK,' said Will. 'I just didn't expect to see so *many*!'

There were rubber fleshblobs hanging on racks, rubber fleshblobs lining the walls and a couple of rubber fleshblobs dangling from the ceiling. There were even a few displays with rubber flesh-blobs arranged in funny positions like dancing teachers and a nanny pyramid.

'If it's too freaky I can always come back another time,' Urk suggested.

'No, I'm fine,' said Will, prodding a nearby dinner lady. This model came with a hairnet that guaranteed *not* to stop hairs falling into food, and a free recipe for lumpy custard.

Once he got over the shock, Will

DISGUSTING DORIS

DREADFUL DINNER LADY DELUXE!

found the store was actually really interesting. So while Urk browsed through a rack of Naughty Kid suits, Will explored the rest of the shop.

The fleshblob accessories section was particularly fascinating; here you could not only purchase clothes and shoes, but also pick up a spare arm or replace a missing eyeball.

Above a basket full of half-price and discontinued body bits, Will saw a noticeboard covered in business cards offering rubber repairs. Among these were also notices from customers seeking rare spare parts and scare partners. In the centre of the board there was a notice that immediately caught Will's eye and almost made him shriek again.

Will looked around to make sure no one was watching and then stabbed the board with his right fork, skewering the

notice on the end. Then he quickly hurried off to find his friend.

Urk was busy with a sales assistant whose nametag said 'Hi, I'm Moop!'

Moop was holding up two unattractive rubber children and pointing out the benefits of fleshblob suits with ugly faces. Will tapped Urk on the shoulder and passed him the piece of paper.

Urk read the notice and immediately grinned. 'I *told* you we'd think of something!' he said excitedly.

'What have we thought of?' asked Will,

who was pretty sure he hadn't thought of anything. But his friend simply winked and turned his attention back to the assistant, who was still trying to sell him one of the ugly children.

'. . . and the best thing about these,' Moop continued, 'is that they're *so*

incredibly ugly you can perform daytime scares with very little effort. All you have to do is creep up from behind and the face will do the rest!'

'They are pretty revolting,' said Urk, scratching his chin thoughtfully. 'But I've changed my mind. Can I have a look at a Mumsy suit instead? Preferably one with orange hair and freckles?'

Moop rolled his eyes, dumped the child suits back on the rack and scuttled to the other side of the store.

'You're not planning to actually *meet* with this Snotgobble?' gasped Will as they followed the assistant. 'The *Monsterbook* said Goopsnottles are very aggressive and territorial, and lots of other bad stuff about bogeys and bombs!'

'It also said they *always* work alone,' said Urk, waving the notice in the air. 'Which means Snotgobble must need a mum for something *really* important. And if we can find out what that is . . .'

'Parents' evening!' gasped Will. 'My school has been holding parents' evenings all this week! My year had theirs yesterday, so the Goopsnottle must be having his tomorrow!'

'Even better!' said Urk, stopping for a moment to explain his plan of action. 'If I volunteer to go along as his mum, all we have to do is think of a way to get the bogey bully thrown out of school!'

'*Sounds* simple enough,' Will frowned.

'That's because it is,' said Urk. 'What could possibly go wrong?'

When the pair caught up with Moop he was pulling out a tall fleshblob suit with a shock of frizzy orange hair. Will and Urk eyed the freckled Mumsy up and down and exchanged confused glances.

'Er, isn't she missing something?' said Urk, frowning at the empty space below the dress where the legs should have been.

'You're not tall enough for an adult all-in-one,' scoffed Moop, reaching into a large barrel containing legs on sticks and pulling out a matching pair. 'So you'll have to use leg-stilts.'

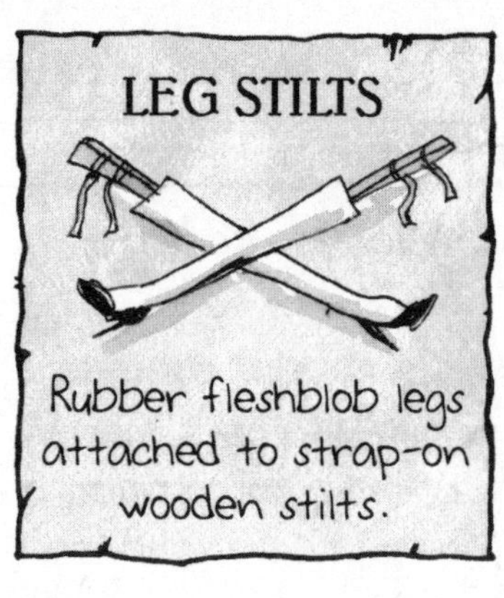

Urk and Will took the suit to the checkout where the young monster charged it to his parents' Monster Mall account, and then registered his fleshblob identity.

Registration included a photo ID with

Urk *and* the Mumsy, and a leaflet called 'You and Your Fleshblob Suit', which Urk slipped into the *Monsterbook*.

5

Wonky Woods and Creepy Caves

Urk and Will left Monster Mall with the top half of a Mumsy suit and two rubber legs and headed straight for the Creepy Caves where Snotgobble lived. The young monster knew a short cut through the Wonky Woods, so the pair had spent the past half-hour clambering through an eerie landscape of crooked stems.

'Did you hear that?' asked Urk, peering back through the misty gloom.

'Hear what?' asked Will, gripping the leg-stilts to use as a weapon.

'I thought I heard fungus being squashed behind us,' said Urk.

Will had been jumpy all the way

through the peculiar little wood and was relieved when he saw light up ahead and the fungus finally beginning to thin out. Then the pair both heard a very loud squelch in the distance and ran the rest of the way.

WONKY WOODS

A small wooded area of tall, thin fungi that have grown so tall they bend all over the place. Small monsters have to weave around the crooked fungi, while large monsters can stomp a clear path straight through the middle.

'Can you even walk on stilts?' asked Will as they hurried into the open.

'I think we're about to find out,' said Urk, and nodded ahead.

Creepy Cave Mountain rose out of the ground like a giant termite mound with zigzagging steps leading to large entrance holes. But standing in the way of that was a narrow brown lake.

'What is it?' asked Will, thinking the water looked a bit odd.

'It's a worm lake,' said Urk.

'The lake has worms in it?' asked Will,

stepping up to the bank.

'No, the lake is *made* of worms,' warned Urk. 'I wouldn't get too close.'

'Oh, I don't mind worms,' Will shrugged, and then quickly jumped back when one of the creatures popped its head out from the squirming mass and snapped at his ankles.

'Those are Nibble Worms, which means they have teeth,' said Urk. 'They've eaten every bridge that's ever been built over them, so the only way we're going to get across is on the stilts.'

WORM LAKE

The world of monsters has grown from a few small dwellings into the glorious Monsterland we know today. This took a lot of digging, and a lot of digging means a lot of homeless earthworms.

Holes were dug all over Monsterland and the worms were thrown in. Over time the worms grew to like their new homes, and evolved teeth to protect them.

NIBBLE WORMS: Nibble Worms can deliver a nasty nip to small monsters attempting to cross a worm lake – while large monsters can simply stomp across, squashing worms in their wake.

Urk sat on the bank of the worm lake out of nibble range and tucked the folded Mumsy suit into his rucksack. Then Will fastened the straps of the leg-stilts to the monster's hooves and helped him stand upright.

Urk was now twice the height of his friend and looked very peculiar as he took a few practice strides up and down the bank, occasionally grabbing a nearby fungus tree to steady himself.

Once satisfied that they were not about to become worm lunch, the pair approached the lake.

'I'll get in first,' said Urk, holding on to Will's head for support as he swayed back and forth. 'That way I'll sink low enough for you to jump on my shoulders, but hopefully not low enough to get nibbled.'

'Then what?' asked Will.

'Then we walk to the other side,' said Urk.

Will steadied the young monster as he plunged his lady legs into the lake, and was relieved when the wriggling worms

only came up to the rubber knees. Then he leapt on to Urk's back and the pair shrieked when they sank further down.

'Hold on tight!' said Urk, moving away from the bank with energetic strides.

Will held on tight by hooking one of his forks under the strap of the rucksack, and used the other fork to fend off the more gymnastic worms that took to the air, snapping their jaws aggressively.

'Can you remind me why we chose the short cut again?' asked Will, flicking off a small worm that had harpooned itself on to the end of his fork.

'Because we don't want anyone else taking the mum job,' Urk grunted, ploughing on through the squirming depths. 'We have to get there first. Although I confess I didn't realize the lake was quite so deep!' he added as the worm level crept up his rubber thighs.

'Well, it's too late now,' said Will.

'What do you mean?' Urk gasped.

'We're more than halfway across!' said Will, glancing over his shoulder.

When Urk looked back and saw how far they'd come, he focused on the last few metres ahead and waded forward with all his might. The worm lake was only narrow, but it took all of his strength to finish the final bit.

As they reached the other side, Will leapt on to the bank and pulled Urk out after him. The young monster frowned at the state of his stilts as he unfastened the straps. The stockings were peppered with little bite holes and the shoes looked as though they'd run a marathon.

'Phew!' said Urk.

'Phew!' said Will.

Once they caught their breath, Urk and Will made their way up the Creepy Cave Mountain steps and quickly found the entrance that led to grottos numbered ten to fifteen. Snotgobble lived in grotto thirteen, and the pair hoped the number would only turn out to be unlucky for the Goopsnottle.

Moving through the dark, damp tunnel, Urk kept stopping to look back the way

they'd come. As with the Wonky Woods, the young monster had a terrible feeling they were not alone.

'Did you hear that?' he asked.

'What?' asked Will.

'I thought I heard footsteps behind us,' Urk frowned.

'It could just be an echo,' said Will.

'I hope not!' gasped Urk, and carried on walking.

The Creepy Caves certainly lived up to their name, with dripping walls, sinister corners and Things scuttling about underfoot.

ECHOFLAPPER

Echoflappers stalk caves in search of host hairdos. They are completely blind and get their name from following sound echoes to track down likely victims.

Echoflappers are very small and nestle into your hair or fur. The only way to get rid of them is to cut the hair off and hope they haven't laid eggs.

ECHOFLAPPER EGG BEATER

Beat those little Echoflapper eggies away!

Urk kept his head low and looked out for low-flying Echoflappers, while Will looked out for anything else that might be lurking in the darkness.

The pair were surprisingly relieved when they arrived at number thirteen.

'You'd better let me do all the talking,' said Urk, pulling out the Mumsy suit and draping it over his arm. 'There's a chance he could recognize your voice from the playground.'

'Fine by me,' said Will.

Urk nodded, took a deep breath and knocked on the door.

6

Snotgobble

Caves are pretty sturdy places to live, being made entirely of solid rock. So it was not a good sign when the floor began to quake with stomping footsteps approaching from inside. Urk and Will immediately leapt back as the large door flew open.

'WHY DID YOU WAKE ME?' roared Snotgobble, filling the space where the door had been. 'I'LL SQUASH YOU INTO . . . INTO . . .' The Goopsnottle scratched his head while he tried to think

of something suitably squashy. Snot would have been the obvious choice – but the monster was clearly still half asleep.

Urk and Will looked at each other as the awkward silence stretched out, then Urk quickly pulled out the 'WANTED' notice and waved it in the air like a white flag of surrender.

'Er, Mr Snotgobble?' he said meekly. 'I would like to be your Mumsy!'

The Goopsnottle's drowsy gaze drifted from the ceiling and rested on the visitors, at which point Urk unfolded the fleshblob suit and Will waved the leg-stilts.

Snotgobble's frown deepened as this new information dribbled into his sleepy brain, then he stomped back into the cave scratching his bottom. He left the door open, which Urk and Will took as an invitation to follow.

The inside of Snotgobble's cave was very similar to the outside, with dripping walls, sinister corners and Things scuttling about underfoot. One side of the cave was obviously the bedroom, because there was something brown and bed-shaped dumped in the corner. The other side had a wall of cupboards stuffed with crisps, biscuits and chocolate bars stolen from the playground.

Will looked around and saw a limp Terrible Tyler suit hanging on the back of the door, and on the floor beside it was a large tub of Toad Fat.

TOAD FAT

Most monsters are larger than humans and lather themselves in Toad Fat to squeeze into a fleshblob suit. Giant monsters have to actually shrink their bodies using Shrivel Salts!

The fleshblob suit was half the size of the Goopsnottle and the boy had a horrible image of the greased monster squidging himself into the suit.

'I'm currently running a very successful school bullying scam,' said Snotgobble, swinging his trunk in the direction of the food store. He snatched a bag of crisps from the shelf, ripped it open and tipped the contents into his mouth. 'And I need a

mother for parents' evening tomorrow, to make sure my cover isn't blown.'

'I'm your monster!' Urk said confidently, holding up the Mumsy suit.

'Well, you're the only one who responded to my notice,' sniffed the monster, eyeing the suit with disgust and twanging the end of its rubber nose. 'So I suppose you'll have to do.'

'Wonderful!' said Urk. 'What's the plan?'

'We will meet at six o'clock tomorrow evening,' said Snotgobble, still chomping noisily on the crisps. 'You'll take me to see my teachers and pretend to care about whatever stupid things they say. Tell them what a little angel I am and make a big fuss of me. Is that understood?'

'You're my little angel,' said Urk. 'Got it.'

'Everything must go smoothly,' warned the monster. 'I don't want any hiccups!'

'No hiccups,' said Urk, and watched nervously as he moved over to Will.

'And who's this little rag?' sneered Snotgobble, showering Will with crisp crumbs as he loomed over him. 'The school only requires *one* parent to attend. I'm not paying for a dad as well!'

The boy peered up at the Goopsnottle and swallowed hard beneath his disguise.

'Er, this is my personal assistant!' Urk said quickly, remembering that he'd told Will not to speak. 'He carries my legs around and stuff like that. I will split my fee with him, of course.'

'On the subject of your fee,' said Snotgobble, moving back to the shelf and gathering a small selection of goodies. 'I'm willing to pay one pack of Lumpy Bix, two chocolate Yummy bars and a bag of Cheezy Loo Loos.'

Urk considered haggling for a few extra Yummy bars, because they were his favourite fleshblob snack, but decided not to push his luck. 'That will be acceptable,' he said as the Goopsnottle dumped the food into Will's arms.

FLESHBLOB SNACKS

Fleshblobs are of course a putrid waste of space and should be made to wee their mattresses all day long. However, their snacks are very tasty.

Snotgobble was about to speak again when the boy began making grunting noises that he hoped sounded like a disapproving Jub Jub. Urk looked over and saw his friend prodding the Lumpy Bix and Yummy bars with a fork.

'Er, we appear to be missing a bag of Cheezy Loo Loos,' said Urk, gathering the biscuits and chocolate bars from Will, who was barely managing to hold the leg-stilts in his forks.

'You'll get those when the job is done and I'm satisfied with your work,' said Snotgobble, grabbing a bag of Cheezy Loo Loos with his trunk and dropping it into his school bag. 'Wait

for me outside the school gates at six, and *don't* be late.'

'Six o'clock, St Margaret's Elementary School,' Urk confirmed, and nodded in an official manner. 'I'll be the one with the frizzy orange hair,' he added, patting the head of his fleshblob suit.

The Goopsnottle grunted and made his way back towards the bedroom area of his cave, which seemed to mark the end of the meeting. Urk and Will exchanged shrugs and then hurried for the door.

The pair only made it halfway across the murky cave when the floor began to quake again as Snotgobble suddenly barged past them. He slammed the door shut and blocked the exit further by pressing his bulk against the wood.

‘How did you know which school it was?’ he growled, picking a large bogey from the end of his trunk and rolling it around his fingers in a threatening manner. ‘I don’t remember mentioning that it was *St Margaret’s Elementary.*’

Urk and Will froze like startled rabbits.

‘Well?’ said Snotgobble, adding more

bogeys to the rapidly growing ball.

Will glanced around for another exit and his gaze fell on the rubber Terrible Tyler head peeping over the Goopsnottle's shoulder. He casually leaned closer to Urk and whispered something in his ear.

The young monster glanced up and then addressed the Goopsnottle.

'I've done a lot of Mumsy work, as you can see by the state of my lady legs,' Urk explained, waving a hand at the tatty stilts. 'I know *all* the schools in the area and saw your fleshblob suit was wearing a St Margaret's Elementary School scarf.'

'Oh,' said Snotgobble, and popped the bogey ball into his mouth.

'Six o'clock, then?' said Urk, tapping his hoof impatiently.

'Six o'clock,' grumbled the monster, stepping aside and opening the door.

Urk and Will held their breath as they stepped casually out of the cave and gasped with relief when the door finally closed behind them. Then they legged it as fast as they could out of the Creepy Caves.

7

The Labyrinth of Peril

'I don't think the legs will survive another trip across the worm lake,' said Urk as they reached the base of the Creepy Cave Mountain. 'And we're in no hurry, so we might as well take the long way back.'

'Sounds good to me,' said Will, with obvious relief. 'So how *do* we get back?'

'Through THE LABYRINTH OF PERIL!' Urk roared dramatically.

'What?' Will gasped. 'That sounds even *worse* than the worm lake!'

‘I know,’ laughed Urk. ‘The name is a bit misleading.’

‘So it’s not a perilous labyrinth?’ asked Will.

Urk paused for a moment, pulled out the *Monsterbook* and flicked to the ‘Horrible History’ section. When he’d found the page he was looking for he passed the book to Will.

EARWAX BERYL

Earwax Beryl was one of our more peculiar monsters, having never frightened a single fleshblob. Instead she used her long fingernails to steal their earwax while they slept.

Beryl did this every night for seventy years, built a whole earwax labyrinth and filled it with peculiar earwax sculptures.

THE LABYRINTH OF PERIL
Beryl was of course completely mad, but the Labyrinth of Beryl was a disgusting work of art and opened to the public. No one came because it didn't sound very interesting, until the name was changed to the Labyrinth of Peril, and monsters flocked to see it.

By the time Will had finished reading the tale of Earwax Beryl, the pair had arrived at the Labyrinth of Peril. The entrance loomed above them like a grisly orange fortress.

'I think that's the most disgusting thing I've ever seen,' Will gasped.

'Thanks,' said Urk, and led him through the archway.

As they wandered down the knobbly

orange walls, passing knobbly orange sculptures, Will had to admit that the Labyrinth of Peril was pretty amazing. It also seemed to go on forever!

The boy was wondering if a sculpture of a knobbly orange lump was the same sculpture of a knobbly orange lump they'd passed a few minutes ago, when Urk suddenly stopped and grabbed his arm.

'What's up?' asked Will.

'Shhh!' whispered Urk, tilting his head.

A very faint stomping sound could be heard in the distance, pausing at regular intervals as the unknown creature chose different paths through the maze, and growing louder with every twist and turn.

'Something is *definitely* following us!'

Urk whispered. 'It tracked us through the Wonky Woods, it was lurking close behind us in the Creepy Caves, and now it's followed us here!'

'And I think it's gaining!' said Will as the waxy walls began to tremble.

Urk and Will ran through the labyrinth as fast as their legs would carry them, with the young monster yelling directions whenever they reached a junction. But no matter how fast they ran, the stomping footfalls were never far behind, and the earwax lumps tumbling from the walls told them it was something big.

'Up ahead!' yelled Urk, spotting a tall archway similar to the entrance. 'That *has* to be the exit!'

The pair charged down the orange passageway with all their might and leapt through the arch, but instead of leaping out of the labyrinth, they leapt *into* the enormous knobbly fountain at its centre.

Fortunately the liquid earwax that once flowed from the fountain had long since hardened into a peculiar waxy bloom.

*Un*fortunately, a large shadow was now looming over them.

'Caught you!' it chuckled. 'You little Goo Goo bugs!'

'Miffni!' Urk and Will gasped together.

'That's my name,' she sneered. 'Don't wear it out.'

As the pair clambered out of the fountain they were only slightly relieved to discover their mysterious stalker was Miffni, Urk's massive little sister. Will had met her before and knew she was a worse bully than Terrible Tyler!

'What are *you* doing here?' Urk demanded, brushing earwax crumbs from his fur.

'I still think you're up to something,' Miffni said flatly. 'So when Mum said you were going off to buy a fleshblob suit, I decided to wait outside the Monster Mall and follow you!'

'But you've already got me taken off nightly scare training!' said Urk.

'That was just for starters!' snapped Miffni. She snatched the pack of Lumpy Bix from her brother's rucksack and waved it at him. 'Now I've got proof that you're wandering around Monsterland scoffing stolen snacks with your silly friend.'

'For your information I just got a job with a very nasty Goopsnottle!' said Urk, pulling out Snotgobble's notice and handing it to his sister. 'And he's *paying* me in fleshblob snacks.'

'That's what you were doing at the Creepy Caves?' said Miffni, clearly disappointed after reading the notice. 'And he's actually *paying* you to pretend to be his mum?'

'Yeah,' said Urk, waving his new fleshblob suit ID card at her. 'I think Mum and Dad will be *very* pleased.'

Miffni screwed up her face while she tried to think of something else to accuse him of. Then her gaze fell on Will, who was standing behind her brother fiddling nervously with his forks.

'Why were you explaining monster

things to the Jub Jub?' Miffni said slowly. 'I saw you take out your *Monsterbook* a few times. You explained the worm lake, which is ancient history, and you had to tell him about the Labyrinth of Peril, which is really famous . . .'

'Willijub is from the Outer Regions,' Urk interrupted. 'He's still learning stuff.'

'Even monsters from the Outer Regions know about *worm lakes*,' said Miffni.

'Er, he's also a bit stupid,' Urk added, and gave Will a nudge.

'Duh?' said Will and scratched his head with a fork. This was quickly followed by a very loud 'OUCH!' as the fork accidentally jabbed his ear. Luckily this made the display of stupidity even more convincing.

'Oh, you're *both* stupid,' sneered Miffni, pulling open the packet of biscuits and stuffing half the contents in her mouth. 'But thanks for the free snacks,' she sneered and then stormed back through the labyrinth.

'That was close!' Urk whispered, dusting off the fleshblob suit.

'Too close,' said Will, pulling the leg-stilts out of the fountain.

'Though it's not like Miffni to give up so quickly,' Urk frowned.

'Then we'd better keep an eye open for her,' said Will as they headed away.

8
The Snot Plot

Urk and Will quickly found their way out of the maze and headed back through the Monsterland tunnels, making sure not to discuss anything regarding the bogey bully and keeping a constant lookout for lurking sisters.

While he was looking out for a lurking Miffni, Will saw lots of other lurking monsters that he'd never noticed before in Monsterland. And with the help of the *Monsterbook*, Urk explained about a mysterious group of monsters known as Lurkers.

LURKERS

Lurkers come in all shapes and sizes and no two are ever the *same*. The one thing they all have in common is their ability to lurk. Lurking involves creeping around without being seen and making fleshblobs feel like they're being watched. This is particularly effective in dark alleyways and tunnels.

EYEBALLS: The most you will ever see of a lurker is eyeballs in the darkness!

Halfway down the Highland Road tunnel the pair stopped at a shadowy rectangle with '33' scratched in the mud and looked around for Miffni.

Once certain that the coast was clear they shuffled through the hidden doorway into Will's wardrobe and out the other side.

THE TUNNELS

The Monsterland tunnels are named after the street and house numbers above like a giant muddy map.

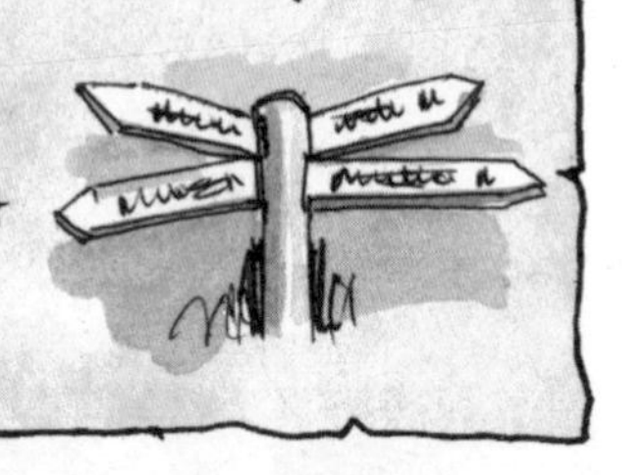

Safely back in his room, Will took off the Jub Jub disguise and kicked off his muddy trainers. Then he helped Urk hang the Mumsy suit on the wardrobe door and propped the leg-stilts against the wall.

'So, what do we do now?' asked Will, realizing they still didn't have a plan.

'The first and most important thing we have to do,' said Urk, rummaging in his rucksack, 'is to eat a Yummy bar!' He handed Will one of the chocolate bars the Goopsnottle had given him.

'That's a very good idea,' said Will, tearing open the wrapper. 'Then what?'

'Then we have to decide on the best way to deal with Snotgobble at parents' evening,' said Urk, chomping through the chocolate at monster speed. 'A clever plot to bring about the downfall of the bogey bully!'

'A Snot Plot!' said Will, thinking a snappy name would be a good start.

Urk nodded and pulled the *Monsterbook* from his rucksack. The book contained everything a monster needs to know about other monsters, and he felt certain the answer was somewhere within its grisly pages.

'It should be easy to get him kicked out,' said Will, finishing off his last chunk of Yummy bar. 'Especially with you playing the part of his mum; you could just pull him out of school.'

'That would work,' said Urk. 'But then he'd just move on to *another* school.'

'That's true,' said Will, who wanted the bogey bully gone, but not if he was bullying some other bunch of kids. 'So we also have to make sure he can't start up somewhere else?'

'Yeah,' said Urk, drumming his fingers on the *Monsterbook* cover.

'What if we stole the suit?' suggested Will.

'That would rid us of Terrible Tyler,' said Urk. 'But Snotgobble could just report it missing and register a new fleshblob identity. A Rotten Richard or a Dreadful Daniel, and then we wouldn't know who to look out for.'

'Why do you have to register fleshblob identities anyway?' asked Will, who had wondered about Urk having his photo taken when he bought the Mumsy. 'It seems a bit strict, all that fuss for a rubber costume.'

'Oh, there are lots of rules and regulations with fleshblob suits and daytime scaring,' Urk explained. 'Most of it is there to make sure monsters don't pop out in front of grown-ups.'

'Pop out?' Will gasped.

'Revealing their true monster appearance,' said Urk. 'That can get you a lifetime ban from ever owning another fleshblob suit. It's one of the worst things a monster can do because we rely on grown-ups not believing in us.'

'A lifetime ban?' Will smiled. 'That's interesting.'

'Yes,' Urk smiled back. 'That's *very* interesting.'

There was a moment of silence where the boy and the young monster wondered what to do with this new information, then Urk grabbed the *Monsterbook* and flicked through its pages until he found the leaflet he'd been given with the suit.

YOU AND YOUR FLESHBLOB SUIT

Fleshblob suits are a fun and easy way to move around in the world of fleshblobs during the day. Once on the surface you can menace as many fleshblobs as you want, but you must abide by the conditions of use:

1. Never wear your fleshblob suit in Monsterland or you might get eaten by another monster. Look in the A–Z of Hidden Doorways to find entry points with a changing cubicle.

2. Always keep your fleshblob suit in good repair. Real fleshblobs DO NOT walk around with holes, tears and limbs hanging off. It is very important that you look convincingly fleshblobby at all times.

3. Never reveal your true monster identity in the presence of a grown-up. Punishment for breaking this rule is a lifetime ban, which means:

YOU WILL NEVER BE ALLOWED TO OWN A FLESHBLOB SUIT AGAIN!!!

'Then it's decided!' said Urk, slamming the book shut excitedly. 'We have to rip his head off!'

'That seems a bit harsh,' frowned Will.

'Not his *real* head, silly,' laughed Urk. 'His *fleshblob* head.'

'But you said monsters rely on grown-ups not believing in them,' said

Will. 'If all the parents and teachers see Snotgobble's big ugly head, they'll know monsters are real and the whole of Monsterland will be in trouble.'

'You'd think so, wouldn't you?' said Urk. 'But when monsters *do* get spotted, adults always come up with an explanation for it. They see what they want to see and then fill in the gaps with something more believable.'

'Then why have the rule at all?' asked Will.

'It only works if sightings don't happen very often,' Urk explained. 'If adults saw monsters regularly they wouldn't be able to explain it away. The rule is there to keep monster sightings to a minimum.'

'I'd like to know how the teachers will explain away Snotgobble!' said Will.

'They'll think of something,' said Urk. 'You'll see.'

'So how are we going to pull his head off?' asked Will.

'You'll have to sneak up from behind and grab it,' said Urk matter-of-factly.

'Me?' Will gasped.

'Well, I'll be playing Snotgobble's mum, so he'll be watching me the whole time,' said Urk, jabbing a thumb at the rubber Mumsy hanging from the

wardrobe door. 'He won't recognize you without the Jub Jub disguise, so you'll be able to get really close.'

'I guess you're right,' Will sighed, and then said something he thought he'd never have to say in his lifetime. 'That means I'll have to think of a good excuse to stay late after school . . .'

9

School Gate Scare

The following day Will stood by the school gates at six o'clock waiting for Urk to arrive in his fleshblob suit. The pair had

planned to meet up before Snotgobble arrived, to run through the Snot Plot one more time.

The plot itself was quite simple. Urk would take the bogey bully into the school hall and meet with the teachers as originally planned, then Will would stay close by and pull the rubber head off the monster when Urk gave the signal.

Will had been waiting for five minutes and Urk was nowhere to be seen.

The school gates were busy with kids and parents coming and going, and the boy was frantically checking his watch. Then he glanced up and saw a tall lady staggering towards him on tatty legs.

'Hello, little boy!' shrieked Urk in a peculiar high-pitched voice. The young monster tottered to a stop and grabbed

Will's shoulder for support. 'Sorry I'm late,' he whispered. 'One of my shoes fell off and it took ages to stick it back on again.'

'It's OK, Snotgobble's not here yet,' said Will, smirking at his friend's strange appearance. Urk still *sort of* looked like

Urk, just a very tall Urk with a pink face and frizzy orange hair. 'Tyler didn't come to school today, so he might not even –'

Will didn't get to finish what he was saying because a very loud voice boomed from the crowd. 'WHERE'S MY MUM?' it yelled, and when the pair turned around they saw Terrible Tyler barging through a small group of parents and kids.

'I volunteered to hand out orange squash,' Will whispered quickly. 'So I'll wait for you inside and look out for the signal,' he added, and hurried away leaving Urk swaying on his stilts.

'There you are, you withered old clam!' yelled Tyler, ignoring the disapproving gasps from nearby grown-ups. 'Now, let's get this thing over with so you can buy me some ice cream!' he added, grabbing Urk's arm and tugging him towards the school.

'Er, whatever you say, poopikins,' trilled Urk, lumbering after the bogey bully.

'Who were you talking to?' hissed Tyler. 'I saw you chatting to a fleshblob.'

'Er . . . I was just scaring that boy,'

Urk said quickly. 'Um, I told him I was a wicked witch looking for children to put in my oven, and he nearly did a wee wee right there and then!'

'I didn't pay you a whole pack of Lumpy Bix to work your own scares,' growled Tyler as they entered the corridor and followed the arrows to the main hall. 'You're here to do *whatever* I tell you! Is that clear?'

'Yes, my little dumpling,' Urk sighed.

'Good. Because I plan to have some fun,' Tyler

added mischievously. 'And you're going to help me.'

'But I thought you said you didn't want any hiccups?' Urk gasped.

'I changed my mind,' said Tyler with a wicked grin.

10

Hiccups and a Familiar Burp

As he entered the hall with Tyler, Urk quickly looked about for his friend. The teachers were all seated at small tables along one wall and there were long rows of chairs with parents and children waiting to be called. Will was hovering around a long table filled with cups and jugs of orange squash, trying to look busy.

'I want a drink!' yelled Tyler, and gave Urk a hard shove with the end of his shoe.

Urk lurched forward and tottered down the hall, waving his arms frantically to stay balanced on the stilts. He was picking up speed as he staggered towards the drinks, but Will managed to grab him by the arm and swing him round before he crashed into the table.

'Something's wrong!' Urk gasped, swaying back and forth.

'What?' said Will, casually handing over two cups of orange squash.

'It's the bogey bully,' said Urk. 'He wants hiccups!'

'Hiccups?' said Will, not knowing what he meant.

'Yeah, and he also said he paid me a packet of Lumpy Bix,' said Urk, struggling to manage the cups and the stilts at the same time. 'But he didn't seem to remember the two Yummy bars or the Cheezy Loo Loos . . .'

Suddenly Tyler appeared beside Urk and snatched the drinks from him. He guzzled them one after another, threw the paper cups on the floor and then jumped up and down on them.

'I'm bored!' he said, and did a massive *BURP*!

The burp was very long and loud like a foghorn and Urk thought it sounded strangely familiar. But before he could place it, Tyler was tugging him towards the teachers' tables.

MONSTER BURP

Burping is very popular in Monsterland and monsters do it with as much length and volume as possible. There are even burping championships and an annual burp holiday.

Will had no idea what Urk was trying to tell him about hiccups and Lumpy Bix, so he decided to stick to the plan and followed them at a safe distance. When the pair sat down at a teacher's table, Will hid behind a potted plant and waited for the signal.

Tyler had dragged Urk to the table of Mrs Kindheart because it was the only one without a parent and child. Mrs Kindheart was anything but kind-hearted and gave a disapproving snort as the pair sat down.

'Hello, Mrs Poo Poo Bottom!' said Tyler.

'I beg your pardon?' shrieked Mrs Kindheart.

'I said "Hello",' said Tyler, smiling sweetly.

'No, what did you say *after* that?' Mrs Kindheart demanded.

'Er, I can't remember,' replied Tyler. 'What *did* I say?'

'Poo Poo Bottom!' said Mrs Kindheart.

'Har! Har! You just said Poo Poo Bottom,' said Tyler, and roared with laughter.

Tyler's laugh was a series of grunts and squeals with an occasional high-pitched wheeze that Urk immediately recognized. He'd heard this laugh many times before, usually when the joke was at his expense.

'Miffni!' he whispered.

'That's my name,' she sneered. 'Don't wear it out.'

'But the fleshblob suit?' Urk gasped. 'How . . .?'

'When I left you at the Labyrinth of Peril, I went back to the Creepy Caves and stole it from the snoring Goopsnottle,' Miffni said, looking very pleased with herself. 'You didn't think I'd give up that easily, did you?'

'No,' Urk growled. 'But why?'

‘Because I *know* you’re up to something,’ she said, narrowing her eyes. ‘So I followed you here, and I have to say I’m surprised you didn’t bring your silly Jub Jub friend with you.’

Urk quickly looked for Will, to warn him not to pull Tyler’s head off. He saw him lurking behind the pot plant and waved frantically. Unfortunately the pair had not decided on the exact signal Urk would give, so Will assumed the waving *was* the signal.

The boy immediately leapt from his hiding place, skidded down the hall towards the table and grabbed a handful of hair as he passed. With a squelch of Toad Fat the rubber mask slid up Miffni’s head and revealed the face beneath, and when Will saw who it was he quickly let go.

That was when lots of things happened at once.

Mrs Kindheart squealed at the sight of Miffni, and Miffni poked her long blue tongue out at the startled teacher. Then Will quickly shot behind Urk's chair and asked the question that both of them were wondering.

'If Miffni is Tyler,' he gasped, 'then where's Snotgobble?'

As if in answer to the question, a thunderous rumbling began to echo through the hall. Mrs Kindheart stopped squealing, Miffni withdrew her tongue and everyone in the hall stared at the centre of the floor.

The floorboards of the hall were beginning to throb and buckle as the rumbling grew louder, and everyone in the area backed away until they hit

the wall. Then there was an enormous explosion of splintered wood as something big and stripy burst through the floor!

11

Snort 'n' Splat

'WHO STOLE MY FLESHBLOB SUIT?' boomed Snotgobble.

The monster's voice was very loud, but could barely be heard over the shrill shriek of terrified screams, the clattering crash of falling chairs and the thudding thunder of shoes charging towards the fire exit.

The Goopsnottle had no interest in the fleeing fleshblobs. He was searching the chaos for a familiar face – and his eyes grew wide when he saw it. The face the

monster was looking for was perched on the top of Miffni's head like a horrible hat.

'Uh oh!' she gasped, and quickly pulled the Tyler mask back down again.

Snotgobble stormed towards Miffni, snorting great balls of bogey into each of his six hands and began rolling them around with expert fingers. The bogey balls quickly grew as more snot was snorted through the monster's trunk, creating six massive bogey bombs!

BOGEY BOMBS

Bogey bombs cannot be stored because pressurized snot is very unpredictable. But Goopsnottles can make a bogey bomb in seconds, and with six hands they can build up a repulsive arsenal in no time at all.

Miffni looked around for a place to hide, but the hall had emptied rapidly. In fact, the only ones left after the mass stampede were Urk, Will and a startled Mrs Kindheart.

As Snotgobble charged towards her, Miffni decided the big hole in the floor was the nearest exit and made a run for it.

But the Goopsnottle took off after her, launching his first green grenade – which sailed over Miffni's head and disappeared down the hole.

'Missed me!' laughed Miffni until she realized what he'd done. The bomb exploded under the floor with a massive *WHOMP*! filling the earthy exit tunnel with gurgling green goo.

Miffni leapt over the hole and headed for the fire exit, hurdling the refreshments table along the way. But as she cleared the cups of orange squash, the second bogey bomb rolled under the table and exploded with a *BOOM*!

Thinking fast, Miffni grabbed a plastic tray and surfed to safety as the snot splat filled the floor. 'Later, loser!' she scoffed, stepping from the tray and sprinting towards the doors.

Snotgobble launched his third bomb, which hit the wall with an enormous *BANG*! But Miffni dived through the doorway moments before the bogey blast and fled into the playground where the hysterical horde of teachers, parents and children were gathered.

The Goopsnottle immediately pursued her, leaving Urk, Will and Mrs Kindheart alone in the hall. The boy and the monster glanced at the teacher, saw that she'd fainted and was drooling down her chin, and so leapt up to follow the chase outside.

In the playground the kids and grown-ups started screaming again as the creature followed Miffni through the crowd. But when the last three bogey bombs sailed through the air and burst in a snot shower over what they thought was Tyler, the kids swapped their screams for applause.

'HOORAY!' they cheered, seeing the bogey bully covered in bogeys.

'I'd better make sure he doesn't eat my sister,' Urk whispered.

'OK,' said Will. 'I'll see you later?'

Urk gave a hopeful nod, hitched up his Mumsy skirt and took off after the mucus-covered Miffni and the snarling Snotgobble, who had now left the playground and were charging across the sports field.

'Oh! My poor little poopikins!' shrieked Urk, flapping his

arms as he passed the other parents.
And thinking fast, he quickly added, 'I'll
never bring you back to this terrible
school again!'

12

School Sewer Shock

That night, Urk stepped from the wardrobe carrying his rucksack.

'BOO!' he said.

'ARGH!' said Will. 'How's your sister?'

'Covered in bogeys,' Urk smirked. 'How's your school?'

'Covered in bogeys,' Will chuckled.

'What excuse did the grown-ups come up with for Snotgobble?' asked Urk.

Will took the evening newspaper from the desk and held it up.

THE

EVENING NEWS

SCHOOL SEWER SHOCK!

St Margaret's Elementary School was terrorized today by a giant alligator that came up from the sewers during a parents' evening. It went after one boy in particular, who experts believe to be the previous owner who flushed the alligator down the toilet in the first place. The children of the school thought they had seen a monster, bless the little darlings, but it was an alligator.

Grown-ups at the scene remember seeing lots of green.

OTHER NEWS

TEACHER RETIRES

After 40 years of teaching Mrs Kindheart suddenly decides to retire. Full story on page 7

'I told you,' Urk sighed. 'Grown-ups only see what they want to see.'

'I guess so,' said Will. 'Any news about Snotgobble?'

'Yes!' Urk gasped, pulling a poster from his rucksack and unrolling it.

'So no more fleshblob suits for Snotgobble,' said Will, and then remembered something even more important. 'But what about you? Do your parents still want you to do some daytime scares?'

'After what

my sister did, they don't want either of us having a fleshblob suit,' laughed Urk. 'And Miffni's been grounded for a month, so I won't have to look over my shoulder for a while.'

'So everything is back to normal?' asked Will.

'Yep!' said Urk, taking up his usual spot on the beanbag in front of the TV.

'I'm back on nightly manoeuvres with the *Monsterbook*, and my parents are looking forward to reading this week's scare report.'

'That sounds like hungry work,' said Will, pulling out his break-time snacks.

And they both burst out laughing.

MICHAEL BROAD
MONSTERBOOK
Pongdollop and the School Stink
MICHAEL BROAD
MONSTERBOOK
Snotgobble and the Bogey Bully

'Of all the books you've written, which one is your favourite?'

My favourite book is *Pongdollop and the School Stink* because it was my first adventure with Urk and Will. I really like that they're both from completely different worlds but are still the best of friends. Pongdollop the Monster was also great fun to write because he's so big and angry and smelly.

'If you couldn't be an author, what would you like to be?'

I would probably be an artist. I like to paint in my spare time and the pictures usually have loads of things going on in them. This way I'd still be able to make up characters and tell stories, and get really messy.

'What's the best thing about writing stories?'

The best thing about writing stories is that there are no limits. You can make absolutely anything happen, all you have to do is imagine it. *Monsterbook* is particularly fun because I get to imagine a whole underground world filled with very strange creatures.

'Your characters have all sorts of incredible adventures – what's the most amazing thing that happened to you at school?'

Nothing very amazing happened at my school. We never had a Werewolf Teacher or a Robot Dinner Lady (that I know of). Sometimes a stray dog would wander into the playground, which was always very exciting. The rest of the time I spent wondering what would happen if alien spaceships landed. I still do!

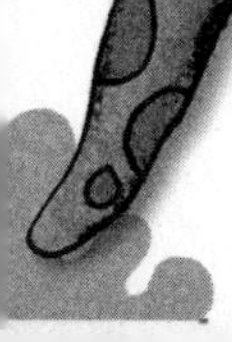

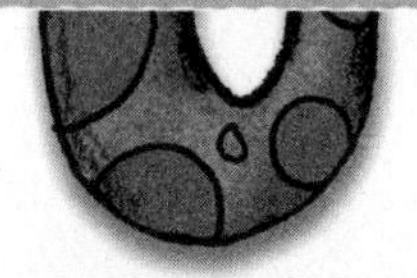

Read all the unbelievable adventures of

JAKE CAKE

that's me ↑

I did all the writing
and all the drawing

puffin.co.uk

Puffin Books